Thomas
and
the
Christmas
Presents

A. VESEY

METHUEN CHILDREN'S BOOKS
LONDON

By the author of
Cousin Blodwyn's Visit
Gloria
The Princess and the Frog

First published in Great Britain 1986
by Methuen Children's Books Ltd
11, New Fetter Lane, London EC4P 4EE
Text and illustrations copyright © 1986 by A. Vesey
Printed in Hong Kong by South China Printing Co.

ISBN 0416 96890 2

for Thomas

It was December.

"Is it nearly Christmas?" asked Thomas.

"Not yet," said his mother. "I still have some shopping to do."

At the shops Thomas's mother bought
presents for all her relations.

Every day the postman bought Christmas cards.
Sometimes there was a parcel.
"Is it for me?" asked Thomas.
"Wait and see," said his mother. "Presents are secret before Christmas."

None of these parcels looks like a bicycle,
thought Thomas.
Thomas was hoping for a bicycle for Christmas.

"Go away, Thomas." said his mother.
"I am wrapping up presents."
"Are they for me?" asked Thomas.
"No," said his mother, "they are not all for
you. Some of them are for your aunt and uncle
and your grandparents. They are coming to
stay for Christmas."

Thomas's mother put all the Christmas parcels away. Some she put in the attic, and some in the cupboard on the landing.

Thomas was in bed, but he couldn't sleep. He was thinking about bicycles. Perhaps there is a bicycle in the landing cupboard, thought Thomas. He had seen his mother put some parcels in there. He decided to look.

Thomas tiptoed to the landing cupboard. His
parents didn't hear him. They were downstairs,
watching television.

None of the parcels *looked* like a bicycle. Thomas opened the biggest one, just to make sure. It was not a bicycle, it was a food mixer.

Thomas opened another parcel.
It was not a bicycle, it was a lamp.
He opened another parcel . . .

. . . and another.

Thomas opened every parcel in the cupboard.
There was no bicycle. Most of the presents were
dull things for grown-ups. The best one was a
large box of chocolates. Thomas ate several from
each layer. Then he sniffed at some bubble bath.

The top would not go back on, and the bubble
bath ran onto the floor.
The landing was a mess. Thomas pushed the
presents and wrapping paper into the cupboard.
Then he went back to bed.

When Thomas was asleep he had a bad dream
about enormous parcels.

Perhaps all that present opening was just
a dream, thought Thomas in the morning.
He rather hoped it was.
"THOMAS!" shouted his father.
"THOMAS!" shouted his mother.
"Come here at ONCE!"

Thomas's father was jumping up and down.
Thomas's mother was slumped against
the cupboard.
"How DARE you, Thomas!" said his father.
"How COULD you, Thomas!"
said his mother.

"I am very VERY angry," said his father.
"There will be no presents for *you*
this Christmas."
Thomas felt very sad.

Thomas helped his mother wrap up the presents
again. The wrapping did not look so good, and in
all the mess and muddle Thomas tied some of the
labels on the wrong parcels.

Then he helped his mother with the cooking . . .

. . . and the cleaning,

and he played with his baby sister.
"Will I really not get any presents this
Christmas?" asked Thomas.
"Some people don't deserve presents,"
said his father.

On Christmas Eve the relations arrived to stay.
Everyone was happy and excited.

"Thomas is rather quiet," said his Grandmother.

At bed time Thomas hung up his stocking.
"Maybe Father Christmas doesn't know I'm
not having presents this year," thought Thomas.
"Maybe he *will* fill up my stocking."

"Father Christmas did come!" yelled Thomas
on Christmas morning.
"Good," said his mother.
"That was kind of Father Christmas,"
said his father.

After Christmas Dinner everyone opened the
family presents round the tree.
Thomas played with the toys from his stocking.

Because of the mixed up labels, some of the
presents were rather strange.
"I have got a box of cigars," said Grandmother.
"And I have got a pink satin nightdress,"
said Grandfather.
"It is not quite my colour." They swapped.

All the presents were opened.
"Thomas," said his father. "I think there
might be something for you in the hall."
It was a bicycle.
"WOW!" yelled Thomas.

"But if you EVER open presents before
Christmas Day again . . ." said his father.
"I won't!" said Thomas.